SPECIAL DELIVERY

Featuring Jim Henson's Sesame Street Muppets

by Valjean McLenighan

Illustrated by
Richard Brown

A SESAME STREET / GOLDEN PRESS BOOK
Published by Western Publishing Company, Inc.
in conjunction with Children's Television Workshop.

Library of Congress Catalog Card Number: 79-57105
ISBN 0-307-23108-9

Ernie was in the kitchen tying up a package.
"Put your finger on this knot, will you, please?"
he said. "I want to make sure the string is good and
tight. This is an important package!"

Ernie pulled out his ink pad and stamped <u>RUSH!</u> on the package in three different places. Next came a <u>HANDLE WITH CARE</u> label, then <u>SPECIAL DELIVERY</u>.

There were so many labels on the package that Prairie Dawn could hardly find the address.

"Pinfeather Falls?" she asked in disbelief.

"Yes," said Ernie. "That's where the Pigeon Fanciers' Convention is held. Bert must be frantic without this, so please hurry, Prairie Dawn!"

"Pinfeather Falls," said Prairie Dawn as she unlocked her bike. "That's quite a trip. I guess the first step is to get downtown."

She hopped on her bike and rode off. Suddenly she heard the thwop-thwop-thwopping of a flat tire.

"Oops!" she said. "No time to fix it now!"

Prairie Dawn got on a city bus and found a seat next to the window.

"There's more than one way to get downtown," she thought.

Suddenly the bus hit a pothole. <u>KA</u>-<u>THUMP</u>!
The package bounced out of Prairie Dawn's lap,
flew out the window, and landed in the back of a
dump truck full of trash.
"<u>Stop</u>!" cried Prairie Dawn.
The bus stopped and she jumped off.

By the time Prairie found a taxi, the truck was almost out of sight.

"<u>Follow that truck!</u>" she said to the taxi driver.

The taxi chased the truck through narrow streets down toward the river. Prairie Dawn could see her package bouncing around on top of the load.

When the taxi turned a corner and pulled up to a dock, the dump truck was already parked and empty.

"It's a good thing Ernie wrapped his package well," said Prairie Dawn as she watched it float down the river on a garbage barge.

Quickly she slipped on a life jacket and jumped into a speedboat at the dock.

Prairie Dawn was halfway to the barge when the speedboat started to slow down. Sputter, sputter! It was out of gas.

Just then she heard a loud noise overhead and looked up to see a hovering helicopter.

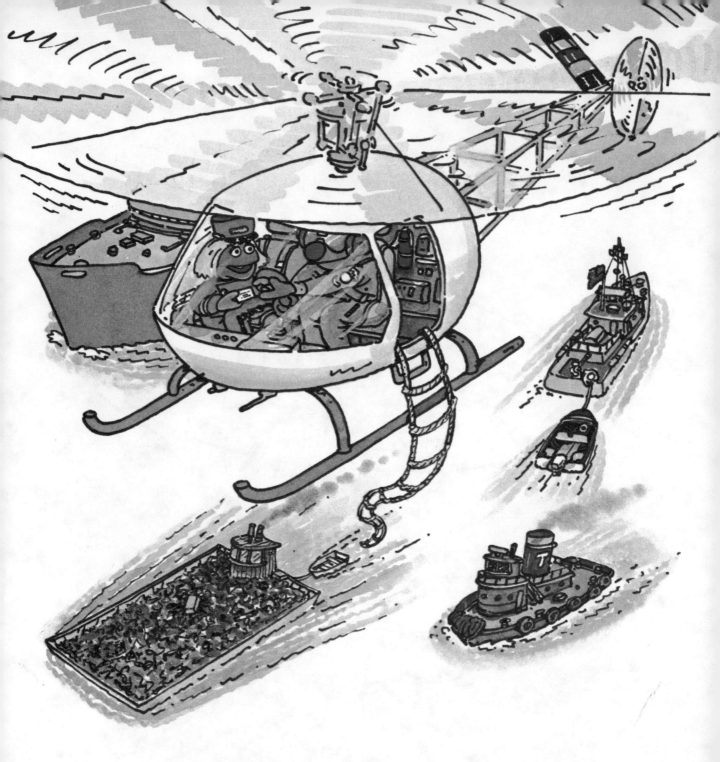

The pilot lowered a rope ladder and she climbed
up into the helicopter.

"Thanks!" said Prairie Dawn to the pilot. "Just
drop me off at the barge, please. And here's my card.
Maybe I can make a free delivery for you someday."

"Do you see what I see?" said the captain of the barge to the first mate.

"Ahoy, there! I'm Prairie Dawn of Prairie Dawn's Delivery Service," she said. "I'm here to pick up an important package..."

"...and there it is!" she cried, snatching the package from the garbage heap.

"I've never lost a package yet," she said, dusting it off. "Now, if I could just borrow your rowboat, please?"

Prairie Dawn got in the rowboat and rowed as hard as she could toward the shore. When she landed, she ran to the train station—and arrived just in time to catch the 4:17 train to Cooville.

"Whew!" she said when she found a seat on the train. Then she took out her map. There were no railroad tracks or roads between Cooville and Pinfeather Falls.

"Goodness," said Prairie Dawn. "It looks as if the only way to get to Pinfeather Falls from Cooville is as the pigeon flies!"

"Did you say Pinfeather Falls?" asked someone from across the aisle.

"Yes," answered Prairie Dawn. "I must get there right away."

"You are in luck. I am Melba T. Burdbrane, president of the Birds of a Feather Company, and I am on my way to Pinfeather Falls. Would you like to ride with me to the Falls?"

So Prairie Dawn and Melba Burdbrane rode to the convention in a beautiful hot air balloon. The Birds of a Feather flock of homing pigeons guided them to a safe landing in Pinfeather Falls.

"Hey, Bert!" called Prairie Dawn, spotting him in a crowd of pigeon fanciers. "I have a package for you from Ernie."

"Good old Ern!" said Bert, ripping open the package. "He knew I forgot something important."

"What?" gasped Bert. "*A picture of Ernie?* Oh, no. I thought it might be my paper clip collection. I don't leave home without it."

"Sign here, please," said Prairie Dawn.